Open and Close

written by Pam Holden
illustrated by Anthony Elworthy

1

This door can
open and close.

3

This gate can open and close.

This window can open and close.

This box can open and close.

This umbrella can open and close.

This book can open and close.

This ca
open an

This mouth can
open and close.

14   16